Drat That Fat Cat!

by
Pat Thomson

illustrated by
Ailie Busby

SCHOLASTIC
PRESS

For Rosalind and Alexandra,
and Grandma too.
P.T.

With very special thanks to Ness.
A.B.

Scholastic Children's Books
Commonwealth House, 1-19 New Oxford Street
London WC1A 1NU, UK
a division of Scholastic Ltd
London ~ New York ~ Toronto ~ Sydney ~ Auckland
Mexico City ~ New Delhi ~ Hong Kong

First published in hardback in the UK by Scholastic Ltd, 2003

Once there was a cat, a fat, fat cat.
But was that cat fat enough?

No,
he was
not!

So he padded along
the path in search of food.

The fat cat met a rat.

"Have you any food, rat?"

"No, I have not," said the rat.

"Too bad, then. I must eat *you* up."

"But you are fat enough already!"

But was that cat fat enough?

No,
he was
not!

So he gobbled up the rat and padded
along the path in search of food, with
the rat going squeak! squeak! squeak!
inside him.

The fat cat met a duck.
  "Have you any food, duck?"
  "No, I have not," said the duck.
  "Too bad, then. I must eat *you* up."
  "But you are fat enough already!"

But was that cat fat enough?

No,
he was
not!

So he gobbled up the duck and padded down the path in search of food, with the duck going **quack! quack! quack!** and the rat going **squeak! squeak! squeak!** inside him.

The fat cat met a dog.
  "Have you any food, dog?"
  "No, I have not," said the dog.
  "Too bad, then. I must eat *you* up."
  "But you are fat enough already!"

But was that cat fat enough?

No, he was not!

So he gobbled up the dog and padded
along the path in search of food, with
the dog going woof! woof! woof!
the duck going quack! quack! quack!
and the rat going
squeak! squeak! squeak!
inside him.

The fat cat met an old lady.
"Have you any food, old lady?"
"No, I have not," said the old lady.
"Too bad, then. I must eat *you* up."
"But you are fat enough already!"

But was that cat fat enough?

No,
he was
not!

So he gobbled up the old lady and padded
along the path in search of food, with the
old lady going Drat that fat cat!
the dog going woof! woof! woof!
the duck going quack! quack! quack! and
the rat going squeak! squeak! squeak!
inside him.

A bee buzzed around the
fat cat's head and, without
a thought, he swallowed it . . .

. . . whole!

The bee buzzed around
the fat cat, where he found
a rat going squeak! squeak! squeak!
a duck going quack! quack! quack!
a dog going woof! woof! woof!
and an old lady going Drat that fat cat!
inside him.

Drat!

Squeak!

"This is an outrage!" buzzed the bee.
"There isn't room to swing a *cat* in here."

The fat cat had forgotten that bees sting.
"Ow!" cried the fat cat.
"Meeow-ow-ow!"

And he got the hiccups.

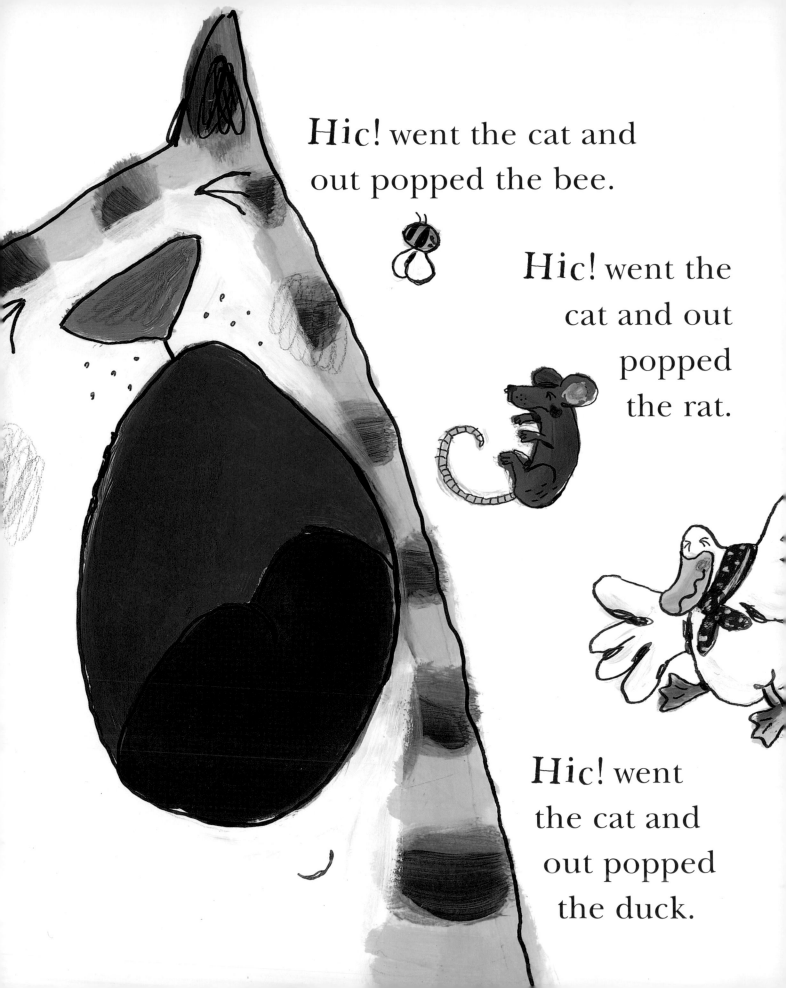

Hic! went the cat and out popped the bee.

Hic! went the cat and out popped the rat.

Hic! went the cat and out popped the duck.

Hic! went the cat
and out popped
the dog.

Hic! went
the cat and
out popped
the old lady.

"Dear me," said the old lady,
"what a very thin cat.
Come home with me
and I'll fatten
you up."

The cat padded along
the path behind her,
in search of food,
going hic! hic! hic!
all the way home.

So was that cat now fat enough?

No, he was not!

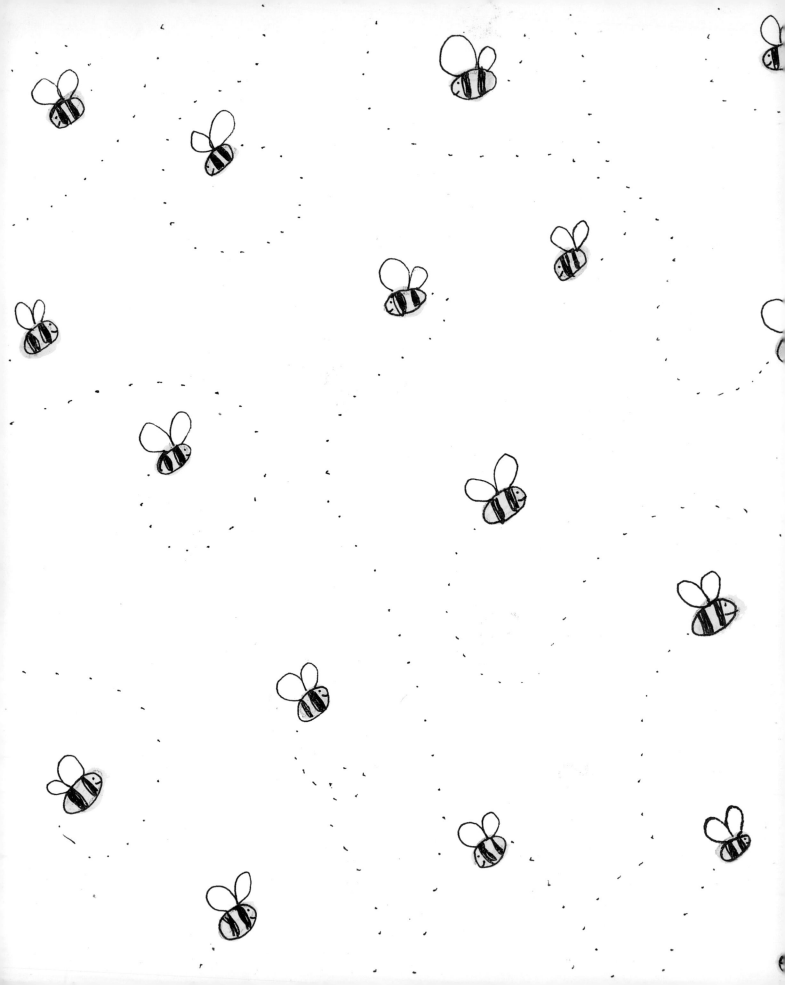